To all the paper boys
that ever were

CHAPTER 1

Joe Riordan concentrated on the rainbow tangle of fiddlesticks on the kitchen table. He'd developed his own theories on how to tell which coloured stick offered the best chance of being withdrawn from the pile without moving any of the others.

Fiddlesticks was the big game that year and most of the kids at Surry Hills primary school had developed some sort of theory about the game. Jimmy Shapcott, for instance, declared firmly that red was the most *slippery* colour and always gave you a better chance than any of the others.

Joe couldn't go along with that; couldn't quite see how one colour could slide more easily than another. But there might be something in it. He was a boy who believed in giving any new idea proper consideration.

In this case he decided on a yellow stick as being the go-er. His three younger brothers and sister watched tensely as he very carefully drew the selected stick out from the tangle. With the tip of the tongue out of the corner of his mouth, he pulled at the stick with infinite care.

'That greenie moved!' cried his brother Andrew.

'No, it didn't,' protested Joe. 'Fair go.'

'It did move! You're cheating!'

Joe was really indignant. 'No, I'm not.'

'Yes, you are! Yes, you are! Mum, Joe's cheating. The greenie moved.'

Their mother's voice from the next room had a fretful edge to it.

'It's got nothing to do with me. You've got to learn to play according to the rules.'

Andrew jumped up and swept the coloured pile of fiddlesticks aside, scattering them all over the table and spilling a few onto the floor.

'I'm not playing with you anymore,' he shouted. 'You cheat!'

'Awww!' protested Joe. 'Fair go!'

The other kids joined in the squabble and all were shouting that he did or he didn't, for one side or the other . . . when suddenly their mother's voice shrieked through the uproar.

'That's enough! For God's sake, I've had enough of your racket. Up to bed the lot of you. Up to bed this instant.'

'Not yet, Mum,' pleaded brother Jimmy.

'It's too early,' whined sister Emily.

'This minute!' shouted Mrs Riordan. It was a voice she seldom used. But when she did the children knew it was time to shut up and do as they were told. They didn't even grumble as they went up the narrow staircase of the tenement house – though they felt injustice had

2

been done. Perhaps Mrs Riordan felt it too, because she carefully did not look up as they climbed the stairs.

Joe, who was last to go, paused in the doorway.

'I gotta finish my homework, Mum,' he said diffidently.

'Very well,' said his mother, but she still refused to look at him.

Joe hesitated, afraid he might be going too far. But when you get to be thirteen – nearly fourteen – and big with it, you're not exactly a kid any more. Particularly when you're the oldest son. You're entitled to ask questions.

'What's wrong, Mum?' he asked gently.

She still would not meet his eye, and her voice was full of tears. 'I don't know where your father is,' she said.

'But he said he was working overtime,' Joe reminded her.

'Yes. That's what he *said*.'

Understanding began to dawn on Joe. 'Where would he be, then?'

'I don't know,' said his mother. 'He said he'd be home at quarter past six. Look at the time now.'

Joe put his arms round her shoulders in a clumsy comforting gesture.

'It's only a couple of hours, Mum. Don't worry. Nothing's happened to him. You bet.'

3

But Joe found it difficult to take his own advice when another hour went by with no sign of his father. He sat at the kitchen table doing his homework, writing in the ruled exercise book with a scratchy steel-nibbed pen that had to be dipped in the ink bottle every couple of words.

His mother was in the easychair in the other room – pretending that she was reading the latest issue of the women's magazine which was a luxury for her at the cost of tuppence every week. A programme of carols was coming over the wireless set that stood on the mantelpiece, even though the Christmas season was yet some weeks away. Not that there was much joy in the season for many people in that Christmas of 1932.

When the front door rattled, Mrs Riordan rose quickly and went down the narrow hallway. The door opened before she could reach it and John Riordan stood on the step, swaying a little as though trying to pull himself together before he entered. He was a big man with a freckled Irish face and red hair showing under a cloth cap. He looked both guilty and resentful.

'Where have you been till this hour?' His wife's voice sounded angry but relieved.

'Getting drunk,' John Riordan said curtly.

She became unnaturally calm. 'Why John? You promised me. What happened?'

'I got the sack, Elsie.'

'Oh my God!' she said.

Unnoticed in the kitchen, Joe felt cold. At this time, in the depths of the Great Depression, these were dreaded words. Even kids knew what it meant when someone got the sack.

'I got a week's pay in lieu of notice,' his father was saying in a dull voice. 'I thought a few drinks at the RSL might make it feel not so bad. I was wrong about that.'

'Only a week,' his wife said.

'Yeah.'

'Only a week's pay,' she repeated, as though she really couldn't comprehend it.

'Yeah, that's right,' said her husband roughly. Then, in a gentler tone, 'They gave me a letter, of course. For what good that'll do.'

'I've got a bit put away,' said Mrs Riordan after a moment or two.

'I calculated that,' he said. 'Reckon that gives us four or five weeks. Just about enough for us to be stony-broke by Christmas. Merry Christmas!'

Somehow that brought the full extent of the disaster home to Joe. The papers were carrying big ads for the festive season and decorations were going up in the shops. Even at that moment on the wireless they were singing the song about decking the halls with boughs of holly . . . and how it was the season to be jolly.

Not for the Riordans it wasn't.

Joe had slipped away upstairs to the bedroom without interrupting his parents. But he couldn't sleep and in the end had to come downstairs again on the way through to the outside toilet.

As he came down, he heard them talking still. The voices were tense and weary, as though they'd gone over and over the problem and found no hope however they looked at it.

'You'll get another job, John,' his mother was saying with an unconvincing note of optimism in her voice.

'It's not just us, Elsie,' said his father. 'It's a world depression. There's millions out of work. I couldn't be lucky enough to crack it for another job. We'll just have to go back to your mother, I suppose.'

'I couldn't stand that,' said his wife despairingly.

'You don't think I'd like it any better, do you? She'd probably teach that rotten parrot of hers to call me a lazy bludger.'

'Maybe we could send the kids to her,' said Elsie Riordan. 'Or at least send the young ones – just till we get on our feet again. Be less mouths to feed.'

'That's a bit of a joke, too,' said John Riordan in a voice far from laughter. 'What the hell are we going to feed any of them on?'

'I could take in washing,' ventured his wife. 'I have before.'

'No. I don't want you to do that.'

'And you could go on the dole.'

'No, I couldn't!' he said flatly. He was a stubborn and proud man and to him there was something shameful in accepting what he saw as charity.

'I think you could, John,' said his wife gently. 'Just consider the situation we're in. What choice have we got? I think you'd better go on the dole and I'd better do some washing and house cleaning.'

There was a long pause from inside the room. But just as Joe was about to tiptoe carefully away, his father spoke again in a voice he didn't recognize for a moment. The way it sounded, Joe was terribly afraid that his dad might start crying.

'It's happened to us, hasn't it, Elsie?' he said. 'You hear of it happening to people all around, but somehow you never really believe it'll happen to you. Just like it was in the war. You and me and the kids . . . I thought we were somehow special.'

'Yes,' said his wife. 'I thought we were sort of special, too.'

Joe stole away, but he carried the thought with him.

Why *them*? Why did it have to happen to the Riordans?

CHAPTER 2

Joe was still asleep the next morning when his mother came quietly in, so as not to disturb the other children, and tried to rouse him.

She shook his foot gently and whispered his name. He murmured in his sleep and turned over, but did not wake. She shook him more urgently and called his name more loudly. 'Joe. Joe!'

He woke blinking in the early light. 'Yes, Mum,' he mumbled unwillingly.

'Please wake up.'

'I *am* awake,' he protested.

His mother pleaded in a whisper. 'Joe, I've got to have a talk to you.' And the tone of her voice brought it all flooding back. His memories of the night before.

'Yeah, of course. I'm awake. I really am.'

'I'll make you a cup of tea in the kitchen,' she said, drawing her faded cotton dressing-gown around her.

'Yeah. Right. I'm coming.'

Mother and son sat at the kitchen table. Joe was still in his pyjamas. He'd never owned a dressing-gown, but used his old overcoat if he needed one, when it was cold, to go to the outdoor dunny at night. But the weather was warm at this time of the year, and he sat there in his striped cotton pyjamas, sipping the strong, sweet tea.

'I hate to ask you, Joe,' his mother was saying, 'but if you could get a job over the Christmas holidays it would be such a help.'

'Well yeah, Mum, of course. But I got the paper round, remember.'

His mother looked a bit shamefaced. 'I've already counted that in. It's not much. If you could get something else it'd be a real help. Maybe we could just make out.'

The weight of responsibility and the dreadful alternative oppressed Joe deeply. 'Cripes. It's not good, is it?'

She was beyond pretence. 'No, it's not.'

'How's Dad?'

She was noncommittal. 'Well, he's still snoring.'

Joe noted the lines on his mother's face. They seemed much deeper than they had been the day before. He was troubled by the thought that came to him, but it had to be faced.

'You wouldn't want me to leave school altogether, would you? Get a fulltime job? Maybe I could swing one – being a kid, like.'

A shadow passed over his mother's face. She had thought of this possibility and the sense of guilt made her quick to protest.

'No, no, of course not! You couldn't do that. I don't want you to, not when you're doing so well and going on to high school next year.'

They looked at one another in silent misery and understanding.

'Have another cup of tea, love,' urged his mother.

'No thanks, Mum,' said Joe. 'Gotta get on my round.'

Normally he felt a deep satisfaction in his morning paper run. It was always a bit of a battle to wake up, of course – always seemed much more inviting to snuggle back in the warmth of bed – but once he was on the round he delighted in it.

At this time of morning the streets looked quite different. Pedestrians were mainly workmen making their way across town on foot or bent on catching early trams or trains. Or down-and-outs who had slept in some alley or similar refuge and were now making their way to join other unfortunates congregating in the parks.

With the streets almost silent you could clearly hear the thump and clatter of carriages and wagons being shunted in the railway yards at

Redfern . . . the great steamtrains puffing along the tracks into Central Station, and the deep warning toot of the steam whistle as they prepared to pull out of the platform again.

The traffic in the streets at this hour was mainly the horses and carts of milkmen and bakers on their early rounds, with an occasional open-sided motorcar or truck.

Joe liked the clear light of early morning and the fresh feeling there was about the air in the hilly little streets crowded with narrow tenements packed close together. He found pride and pleasure in throwing the tightly-rolled papers so that they banged with deadly accuracy right on the doorstep of his customers.

This morning his mind was on other things, but the old skill and instinct still carried him through. His papers were right on target as he rode or wheeled his bike along with its load of papers packed in the wire basket hooked to the handlebars.

A couple of customers were waiting on their doorsteps for him. He answered their greetings automatically, but his mind was still on his problem. At the end of his round he rode back and leaned the bike outside the small shop that housed the newsagency.

Oh well . . . all he could do was ask, wasn't it?

He squared his shoulders and walked inside.

The shop smelt excitingly of ink and paper and was bright with the colours of books and magazines and all the mysterious paraphernalia of stationery. There was also the fascination of the piles of boys' magazines – *Champion* and *Triumph* and *Magnet* and *Comic Cuts*.

But on this occasion Joe scarcely noticed them. He cleared his throat in an agony of embarrassment. 'Huhhrumm. Mr Crabtree.'

The greyhaired newsagent looked up from sorting a consignment of magazines and peered at him intently through his half-moon glasses.

'Anything wrong, Joe?' he asked, concerned.

'Well, yeah. A bit.' Joe shuffled uneasily. 'I was wondering whether there was anything else I could do over the holidays – on top of the paper run – to make a bit of extra money. The exams are over. I could start tomorrow.'

The newsagent peered over the top of his half-moon spectacles and nodded sympathetically. 'I see. Dad got the sack then, did he?'

'Yes, he did.' It was an embarrassed mumble.

'It happens to anyone,' said Crabtree with ready sympathy. He considered the situation for a moment or two. 'Look, there *is* something going. Just I'm not sure whether I should steer you to it or not.'

'I'm big enough,' urged Joe. 'I'd be willing to try anything.'

'Oh, it's only a paper job, you know. Selling in the streets. Just I don't know whether I'd advise you to take it on.'

'Why? Is there something crook about it?'

Mr Crabtree shook his head dubiously. 'Well, the last boy who had the job's in hospital.'

'How'd that happen?'

'He got beaten up.'

There was a considerable pause. Then Joe nodded as though he had carefully weighed up all the information. 'Ah, I see. And how long's he going to be in hospital for?'

'Maybe a month or more.'

'Then the job's going? I could have it if I asked for it?'

'Well,' said the newsagent, 'the job's not actually mine to give. But I know the man you'll have to see. He's a friend of mine and I can give you a reference. But I don't know that I'd be doing you a favour at that. In fact I'd recommend that you didn't take it.'

'Thanks, Mr Crabtree,' said Joe, 'but there's not much choice. Reckon I'll have to take it – if I can get it.'

Clutching his letter of reference like a talisman Joe tracked his way through the loading bays at the back of the newspaper office. The combined smell of paper and ink was one he was familiar with from his morning round; but it was much stronger here and mixed with the stink of petrol fumes from the delivery trucks. There were tatters of paper everywhere, and huge reels of newsprint were stacked along the concrete ramps.

13

Men in inky and oily overalls looked at the name on the envelope Joe carried, and pointed out the way down draughty corridors. After only a couple of wrong turns he found Mr Crabtree's friend.

Mr O'Brien was a beefy, darkhaired man who seemed much too big for the small and cluttered office. He smoothed his luxuriant moustache and looked from the reference to Joe appraisingly.

'Well, you're a good big lad, and that helps,' he growled in an amiable way. 'Old Bill Crabtree says you're a good hand, and he's a man whose word's good. We were in France together, you know, old Bill and me.'

Joe wasn't quite sure what he was supposed to say to that. 'Were you, sir?' he ventured.

'Yep,' said Mr O'Brien. 'We certainly were.' For a moment he seemed lost in deep recollection. Then he shook his head and got back to business. 'You realize you'll be on commission, of course?'

Joe was taken aback. 'No. What's that exactly?'

'Well, the more papers you sell the more money you make. Simple as that.' Then, as he saw the boy was still doubtful, he added reassuringly, 'It encourages private enterprise. It's an incentive.'

'Ah,' said Joe. 'I see.'

But he didn't. Not really.

Some of the harsh reality of it was brought home to him next day when he picked up his ration of papers, along with other sellers, and took up his stand on the pub corner they'd told him would be his pitch.

The cry of the newsboy is traditionally a weird yodelling sort of call that, to the uninitiated, might almost be in a foreign tongue. Joe had heard it often enough and had long envied the virtuosity of those who practised it in the streets.

It sounded like, 'Pye-up! Pye-up! Brewalmurder nazhnl park. Pye-up! Pye-up! Reedawlabartit!'

He was a bit shy about it at first. Selfconscious about making a noise like that in public. But in a few minutes he got into the swing of it, and was just beginning to enjoy himself in fact when a harsh voice behind him snarled:

'And what the hell d'ya think *you're* doing here, mug?'

The ugly interrogator – another newsboy, fully a head taller than Joe – was looking at him in a distinctly menacing way.

'I'm just selling papers,' said Joe, trying to hide his alarm.

'Sell 'em somewhere else,' snarled the newcomer. 'This is my pitch. Git out. Go on, scoot!'

'Fair go. They told me I was right. I was here first,' protested Joe.

But the bigger boy wasted no more words. He dropped his own bundle of papers and,

15

leaping ferociously at Joe, dropped him to the ground with a few experienced and very damaging punches.

'Now git out, mug,' he said. 'Or I'll *really* hurt you.'

Sore and sorry, and there being no help for it, Joe lugged his papers down the block. Around the next corner there was already a newsboy crying his wares – a boy who was a good head shorter than Joe.

Rubbing his swollen lip where the bash-artist had split it, Joe thought he'd learned something about private enterprise.

'Go on, scoot!' he ordered the smaller boy as roughly as he could manage. 'Hop it. Get going!'

'This is my place,' said the small boy bravely.

'Not any more it's not.'

The boy put his papers down on the footpath and raised his small fists. Joe grabbed his opponent's arms and held them despite his vigorous lunging. 'Look, I don't want to fight you,' he almost pleaded.

Near to tears but stubbornly belligerent, the small boy declared: 'You'll have to if you want this pitch.'

'Aw gee!' said Joe. But there was no time for talk as the other boy tore free and launched valiantly at him.

More than half ashamed, but with some vague, sporting idea that it would be kinder to finish it quickly, Joe poked out his left fist to stop him, then hit hard with a right cross. Just like his dad had taught him.

Blood spurted from the smaller boy's nose. He stood there for a moment, dazed, demoralized and bleeding. Then he picked up his papers and walked away, holding his nose and blubbering quietly.

Joe couldn't really feel any pride in his victory – though he tried to tell himself this was the way it was in the streets. Crestfallen he picked up his papers and went into the ritual cry:

'Pye-up! Pye-up! Reedawlabartit! Pye-up! Pye-up!'

CHAPTER 3

It wasn't all that good a pitch. Joe made a bob or two in the lunch hour flurry, but the afternoon was slack and it didn't pick up with the after-work traffic.

Normally the cry he was giving would have had them scrambling for a paper. 'Pye-up! Pye-up! Bradman shock in first test. Pye-up! Reedawabartit!' But everyone coming towards him seemed to have bought a paper elsewhere.

Despite all the people passing by, Joe began to feel a sense of loneliness and isolation in his job. And the only time he did fall into conversation with anyone it wasn't all that much of a success – either socially or economically.

A fairly well-dressed man bought a paper from Joe and as he walked away was accosted by a shabby and unshaven character who had been loitering nearby. He touched two fingers to the brim of his battered slouch hat in parody of salute and said in an ingratiating tone: 'C'd you spare the price of a cuppa tea for an old Digger, mate?'

'No, no,' said the well-dressed man. But apologetically, as though embarrassed by refusing.

The derelict showed a touch of the old larrikin spirit.

'Well, what about a penny to weigh meself, then?' he said cheekily.

'Oh, go away,' said the other man wearily, and walked off down the street.

The down-and-out in the old army hat nodded confidentially to Joe. 'I fought a war for that so-and-so,' he said. 'And look at me now.' He invited Joe to contemplate his shabby gear. 'And look at him.' Together they watched the well-dressed man turn the corner and pass out of sight.

The down-and-out turned to Joe and looked him up and down. 'How are you holding, mate? Would you have maybe a zac to spare for an old Digger that's very near at the end of the road?'

Joe was unwilling, but trapped. Partly it was that the shabby man had spoken to him and appealed to him as a grownup. It was the first time anyone had ever begged from him in an adult way. 'Yeah, sure,' he said. Hating to part with the money, but unable to resist the instinct to charity, he handed over the sixpence.

The man in the battered slouch hat was almost tearful, in a manly way, in his gratitude. 'I'll remember this as long as I live. You mark my words, mate. I won't forget what you done for me at a time when I didn't have a mouthful of food past me lips all day and was faint with hunger.'

He crossed the road and ducked swiftly into the little wine saloon halfway down the block. Joe shrugged, angry and exasperated with himself. Maybe that big kid who had beaten him up had been right. He was a mug.

As evening was falling he realized that he hadn't checked just what time he was supposed to finish working. He jingled his little money-bag to comfort himself and was reluctant to leave his pitch while there was still a chance of selling a few papers.

There was a certain amount of entertainment in the passing parade of the street. Characters went to and from the pub down the road or the wine bar across the street. People dressed up on their way for a night out, old ladies taking small dogs for walks . . . and often the other way round.

When the Salvation Army set up a meeting nearby he enjoyed the lusty singing and the musicians playing with enormous zest on the drums and brasses and the tambourines. He'd noticed that at every Salvation Army meeting they were really great with the tambourine – shaking and rattling it high and low and banging it expertly on elbow and wrist.

Then a dowdy middle-aged woman began testifying. Calling out in a high and fervent voice . . . She had been a drunkard and had neglected her children and beaten her husband – until Jesus came into her life and changed her heart.

It sounded all right but Joe couldn't help suspecting that she was really enjoying it. Putting on an act was how he thought of it. He preferred it when they got back to singing, with the rousing chorus:

Bread of Heaven,
Bread of Heaven,
Feed me till I want no more . . .

Jeez, thought Joe, he could do with a feed himself.

He seized the opportunity to buy a bread roll from the nearest milkbar. He gnawed it with relish. It helped. But not all that much.

As the Sallies finished and marched off singing with the big drum beating and the band playing triumphantly, a shaggy young man set up his soapbox and tried to hold the remnants of the small crowd. He had a fine stentorian voice that echoed down the street and he spoke with passion and conviction.

'Garn! You were too young to know anything about the war,' one of the handful of audience jeered at something he said.

'I know it was a war fought to defend the wealth of the propertied classes with the bodies and the lives of the working classes,' cried the young man. 'I know that, comrades! It was a war fought, like all wars are, to reduce the numbers of the working classes while increasing the profits of the armament kings,

21

the shipping magnates and other war profi-
teers . . .'

By this time the last of his audience – an old
man and his equally elderly wife – were moving
away. He shouted after them, 'You didn't fight
the war for Australia, you fought the war for
them!' But they walked away unheeding.

'Ah, blast it,' he muttered to himself. 'Hardly
seems worthwhile.'

'*I'm* listening,' said Joe.

The young man looked round, suddenly
alert. 'Yeah. Right. Want a pamphlet?' Joe took
one. 'Might be an idea if we had a proper talk
somewhere. Just you and me together.'

'Well, I might as well pack it in now, I suppose,' said Joe. 'Don't expect I'll sell many more
papers this time of night.'

'I'll walk along with you while you check in,'
offered the shaggy young man. 'Jack is the
name, comrade,' he added, putting out his
hand. Joe shook it firmly. 'Joe Riordan,' he
said.

'Despite the mess the world's in, people just
don't seem to care,' said Jack as they walked
along side by side. 'We could do with some
young blood in the movement.'

The following night, while eating the late
dinner that his mother had kept warm in the
oven for him, Joe read some of the communist

literature that Jack had given him after their talk.

His father was seated at the other end of the kitchen table, sullenly demolishing a second bottle of beer. Two of the younger kids were on the floor in front of the fireplace in the adjoining room working at an old jigsaw and young Jimmy was curled up in the lounge chair, writing with a green pencil in a small pad. His lips moved as he painstakingly formed each letter.

'What you doin', Jimmy?' asked his mother, passing by.

'Writing a letter to Santa Claus,' said her youngest son, his face bright with anticipation.

'What are you asking for?'

'A red scooter,' said Jimmy. 'A Malvern Star.'

'Don't bother,' grunted his father in a surly and despondent tone. 'There'll be no Santa Claus for us this Christmas.'

'Shush!' said his wife, shocked. 'Don't say that, John!'

'Well, it's true isn't it?' demanded her husband belligerently. 'No point in deluding the kid about it.'

In the uncomfortable pause that followed, Joe said, 'Christmas is just a capitalist conspiracy, that's what Jack reckons. He says it's designed to make the working classes spend money they can't afford on things they don't need.'

His father looked at him truculently. '*Does* he now?' he asked sarcastically.

23

Joe returned a level gaze. 'Yeah, he does. And I reckon he's right.'

'*Do* you now?' said his father, being elaborately polite and even more sarcastic. 'This Jack's a commo, is he?'

'Yes, he is,' said Joe shortly.

'A communist agitator? A bolshie?'

'Yeah, that's right.'

'And he's got it all worked out, has he? How to make things better?'

'Yes, he has,' said Joe stoutly. 'He says in Russia there's no unemployment. No depression.'

'Yeah, and he's right at that!' His father was triumphant. 'There's no unemployed in Russia because they were all killed off in the great purges and the great famines and the civil war in the twenties, weren't they?' He sat back in his chair and took a swig of his beer. 'Did he tell you about those, son?' he demanded loudly.

'Don't shout, John,' said his wife quietly. 'In front of the kids. It's not necessary.'

John Riordan ignored her and continued in a browbeating tone:

'Tell you about the civil wars, did he? Tell you about the five million dead and the two million in gaol as enemies of the state, did he?'

'No, he didn't,' Joe conceded.

'Well *ask* him!' shouted his father. 'Ask him about the kulaks. And tell him there's no unemployed in Russia because they're all murdered or starved to death or rotting in gaol!'

'You know so much about it, *you* tell him,' said Joe crossly and childishly. But his father was not to be interrupted.

'And point out to him that the only reason he can say the things he says standing up on a soapbox here is because of what he calls the capitalist system. Free enterprise. Under a communist system he'd be rotting in gaol. Or liquidated.' He shoved a pugnacious face forward. 'You know what liquidated means, son?'

'Drunk,' said his wife tartly.

But he ignored her. 'It means tortured to death, that's what!'

Joe wanted desperately to have done with all this. 'Yeah, all right!' he shouted back. 'I'll tell him!'

There was silence. It was as though everyone had suddenly exhausted their passion and anger.

'Hey, Mum,' called Jimmy from the other room, 'how do you spell bicycle?'

His father sprang to his feet and smashed a big fist down on the table. 'It doesn't damn well matter!' he shouted. 'Can't you get it through your thick skulls? There'll be no Santa Claus in this house this Christmas!'

There was a shocked clamour of protest and grief from the younger children as for the first time they really understood what he was saying. Young Emily was crying and wailing over and over, 'No! Oh no! Oh no!'

'Don't listen to your father,' cried Mrs Riordan desperately. 'It'll be all right, children. He didn't mean it. He's just upset.'

Lurching on his way to the outside toilet, John Riordan swung round in the doorway.

'I'm not upset,' he said in a harsh despairing voice. 'I'm facing facts. That's what we've all got to do. Face the rotten fact that there's not going to be any Christmas for the Riordans this year!'

CHAPTER 4

They were hard and bewildering days for Joe as he tried to adjust himself to the new sort of life he had been thrust into; tried to understand what had happened to the family and to absorb and evaluate the new ideas he was coming up against.

He was keeping up his round for Crabtree in the morning and selling papers in the street until late in the evening. And wrestling with new ideas he got from his discussions with Jack and lying awake half the nights worrying. It left him tired and out of sorts.

On the morning round he didn't feel the old delight in the early sights and sounds; and the deadly aim as a paper thrower that he had prided himself on seemed to have deserted him.

Riding along Gill Street, throwing the rolled-up papers, he missed the front door of number twenty-four altogether. Missed so badly in fact that it landed next door in the garden of number twenty-six – which didn't get a paper at all.

'Blast,' he said as he got off and propped his bike against the fence while he went to retrieve the paper.

man with a grey pointy beard so shaped as to give him a strong resemblance to the well-known revolutionary, Leon Trotsky.

There were only about a dozen in the audience, mostly in the front seats of the little hall, but he addressed them as though speaking to a great crowd in some vast square. He spoke eloquently and passionately and though Joe didn't quite follow it all he responded to the rousing sound of it.

'In a true democracy, need and need alone, will decide what a man has; and capacity, and capacity alone, will decide what he does. From each according to his capacity, to each according to his needs!'

Well, that sounded reasonable enough, thought Joe. But there was another matter that was nagging at him and which he got round to when Jack introduced him to the speaker later.

'Comrade Greenfield, I'd like you to meet Joe Riordan. His dad's just lost his job and Joe's got to support his family.'

Comrade Greenfield shook hands and smiled easily.

'Welcome aboard, Joe. Where do you hail from?'

'Surry Hills,' said Joe. And then, stubbornly pursuing his own line, 'My dad wants me to ask you about the kulaks.'

Comrade Greenfield was caught a bit off-balance by this but he smiled again in that easy and professional manner.

'Well, that's a good question. But I think we'd better give you some literature first. Jack, would you get some pamphlets on the agrarian problems in the USSR for Joe? You have a good look at this material, comrade, and then come back and we'll have a proper talk about the kulaks.'

Joe took the pamphlets. That was fair enough, he supposed.

Another indication of his changed interests and attitudes came when his schoolmate, Robbo, bailed him up in the street.

'Hey, Joe. Fair go. Wagging it from school's okay, but what about the cricket game? Where were you this afternoon? We needed you.'

'Jeez!' said Joe, stricken with the enormity of the realization. 'I forgot all about it!'

'Come off it,' said Robbo. 'You don't just forget a thing like that.'

'Sorry, mate. I had something more important to do.'

Robbo couldn't believe what he was hearing.

'Nothing's more important than *cricket*!' he said in a shocked voice.

But Joe suddenly saw something clearly.

'It's all right for you, Robbo,' he said soberly. 'But some of us have got to start growing up.'

And it was with pardonable pride and a secret feeling that he was indeed coming near to that desired but somehow frightening state of adulthood, that Joe arrived home with the first week's pay from his street selling.

His father, sitting at the kitchen table, ignored him when he came in. He had been drinking during the days since he had been sacked. He was sitting now at the table with an empty beer bottle before him, staring sullenly at his glass, which also was empty.

'I'll get your dinner from the oven,' said Mrs Riordan, as Joe kissed her briefly on the cheek.

'Not just yet, Mum,' he said. 'Got something to show you first.'

Carefully he took the money from his pocket and laid it out on the table. A worn ten shilling note, two bright new florins, a shilling, a sixpence and a penny.

His mother's eyes lit up.

'Joe! Fifteen and sevenpence! Oh, that'll help a lot, love.'

John Riordan lurched to his feet. 'Fifteen and sevenpence! Oh yes, that'll help a hell of a lot, won't it?' he cried with fine scorn. 'There's only one damn thing to do with that sort of money. I'll take my share now.'

Before they realized what was happening he had scooped the ten shilling note up from the table and strode heavily towards the door.

'John! John!' cried Mrs Riordan, running to

intercept him. But the door slammed before she could reach him.

The shock had stopped Joe from making any move. He shook his head, amazed and disbelieving.

'He can't do that. He can't just take the money like that, can he?'

But his weeping mother did not answer.

Joe was still sitting at the kitchen table later that night when his father returned. He had a little pile of books and pamphlets and was absorbed in reading them and puzzling over some of the references when he heard his father stumbling on the step and fumbling at the lock.

John Riordan came in, moving clumsily down the narrow hall. The drink hadn't done anything to improve his depression. He stared challengingly at Joe, and at the literature, and snarled, 'What's all this garbage, then?'

Joe's gaze in return was equally challenging.

'It's not garbage. Leaflets and books. And there's stuff about the kulaks in here.'

'*Is* there now?' said his father with elaborately feigned interest.

'Yeah,' said Joe. 'And Lenin said about kulaks that you couldn't make an omelette without breaking eggs.'

'*Did* he now?' sneered his father, steadying himself against the table.

'That's right.'

'Right! Splendid! Good on him!' cried John Riordan, scooping up the literature in his big hands. 'No, that's enough of this bolshie nonsense. And all this garbage is going into the incinerator.'

As he turned towards the door, Joe leapt up and seized his father's arm.

'No, it's not!' he cried. 'You put that back again!'

John Riordan could hardly believe his son's audacity. He tugged his arm away, trying to free himself.

'What d'y think you're doing? Dammit, let me go!' he growled.

'I want to read it and make up my own mind,' shouted Joe.

His father dropped the books and pamphlets, which scattered over the kitchen floor. He grabbed Joe by the shoulders and roared: 'Listen, you! In this house you do as *I* say. You're not going back to those bolshie meetings and you're not reading any more of this muck.'

Joe was trying to break away from his father to pick up the scattered papers. It quickly developed into a struggle, and in his anger and distress, Joe reacted instinctively – he lunged powerfully upward into his father's belly.

With a bellow of pain and anger his father shook Joe. He hurled him back against the wall, just as his mother rushed in shouting 'Stop it! Stop it! Stop it!'

John Riordan propped and looked round in a bemused way. He presented too tempting a target, and suddenly all the worry and humiliation inside Joe erupted into violent anger. He punched as hard as he could, striking him on the jaw and sending him reeling back.

Cursing, his father came back at him, mouthing threats and pounding him with heavy cuffing blows with his open hand.

'Stop it! The pair of you. Stop it!' shrieked Joe's mother, thrusting herself between them.

Father and son stood panting, face to face. Joe's gaze was filled with hatred and contempt, and when he spoke it was not much like a boy's voice at all.

'You're not entitled to burn my books,' he declared. 'And you're not entitled to take my money to get drunk on. I'm supporting this family now, and I can do what I like.'

John Riordan growled with fury. His hands clawed and with murder in his eye he tried to get at Joe. But his wife clung desperately to him, shouting to her son to run, to get out of the way.

By the time the man had freed himself from his wife's frantic embraces and lumbered to the door, Joe had fled . . . away down the little backyard, through the rickety gate and away up the dark lane.

Realizing the futility of trying to follow, John Riordan shouted into the darkness:

'I'll get you when you come back! You'll

soon get cold and hungry and come crawling home. And by God, I'll get you then! You won't last long out there on your own.'

CHAPTER 5

Looking back from the gate, Joe saw the black silhouette of his father in the lighted doorway and heard his shouted threats. He heard his mother's voice frantically calling, but could not make out what she said. He turned resolutely away and set off down the lane.

Trying to ease the turmoil of his mind, and nursing the bruises on his body and an eye that was beginning to puff up and ache, he walked along the steep little streets of Surry Hills . . . into areas unfamiliar to him.

For a start he didn't care where his footsteps carried him; but as he journeyed he became aware of the great number of people who were out in the open in the great city at this time of night.

Women stood alone in dark doorways. Men huddled in alleys and sheltered corners and on the benches and bandstands in the parks. Joe became aware, as he never had been before, of this secret population of the city. The homeless and dispossessed. And with a sudden cold fear Joe realized that he was now one of them.

The effects of a world war, and now the Great Depression had torn apart the orderly frame of society. The desire to work was not enough, now – there just wasn't work available. Families had been evicted and there were thousands of men and women – and children, too – with nowhere to lay their heads.

Half a dozen times Joe had made tentative moves to find some shelter, but each time had been unable to bring himself quite to it. Now he was so tired all he cared about was some sort of refuge. He found a small, unoccupied culvert in a corner of the park and crawled into it.

It was dry and sheltered from the wind, but even though the weather was mild there was enough chill in the night air to make Joe uncomfortable. He curled up and huddled miserably, certain that he could never sleep like this.

But he had dropped off, and had slept so deeply that he hadn't heard the down-and-out who had crawled into the culvert beside him, and who showed his superior training for this kind of life by sleeping with old newspaper stuffed under his clothes and pulled over him.

It was this man's voice that woke Joe, crying out wildly in some sort of nightmare.

'Get out of it, you mongrel,' he was moaning. 'Get out of it! Oh God, why can't you let me be?'

Then Joe must have fallen back to sleep again, because he was woken again by the dawn sunlight slanting in on his face . . . and looked around – puzzled as to his whereabouts at first – to see his companion at the nearby water bubbler.

The man was sipping water and coughing in a strangled, consumptive sort of way. When he turned away to spit, Joe couldn't help but notice that there was blood in it. The man rinsed his mouth at the bubble and wiped his chin with his sleeve.

'Mornin',' he said when he saw Joe was watching him.

'Yeah.' It didn't seem to call for any comment other than that.

The man fumbled in his pocket and said with bitter humour, 'Well, will you join me for breakfast?' He produced and proffered a small and nearly empty paper bag. 'Have a raisin, mate. I believe they're very good for you. All these newfangled vitamins and things.'

'Ta,' said Joe, scrambling stiffly out of his shelter and taking one of the three remaining raisins.

The man squatted on the edge of the culvert.

'Well, we made another one,' he said. 'Another sunrise. That's some sort of achievement, I suppose.'

'Yeah,' said Joe, again for want of anything better to say.

The man was carefully folding the old newspapers that had served as his bedclothes and was tucking them up under the bridgeway across the culvert.

'Not a bad little place for a doss,' he said, eyeing their refuge with an expert's glance. 'Do y' reckon you might be kipping down here again tonight, yourself?'

'Dunno,' said Joe. 'Reckon I might. Got no-where else in mind.'

'Might see you then, eh mate?' said the man diffidently.

'Yeah,' said Joe. 'I got to get going now.'

'Just a tip though, mate,' the down-and-out called after him. 'If you're going to doss here tonight get yourself a lot of old newspapers. Best thing in the world to keep you warm – old papers shoved under your clothes.'

Joe let himself in through the back gate and moving carefully on tiptoe made his way up the yard of the Riordan house.

He took his bike and wheeled it stealthily down the path. The pedal caught and the machine clanked loudly as he manoeuvred it through the back gate. Joe froze and looked apprehensively up at the top windows of the house.

But no one stirred.

Pushing the bundle of papers across the counter, Bill Crabtree noted Joe's black eye and rumpled appearance.

'You okay, Joe?' he asked.

'Yeah, fine,' he replied gruffly.

'No trouble at home?' It was a deliberately casual question.

'No,' said Joe shortly.

Crabtree watched him go with a shrug of resignation. Not much he could do to help anyway.

Halfway through his round he stopped at Robbo's house and carefully flicked a few pebbles of gravel at the second storey window. His schoolmate shoved a tousled head out.

'Can I leave my bike here of a morning?'

'Yeah, sure,' yawned Robbo. 'What's the trouble?'

'Me and me dad had a blue,' said Joe. 'I've shot through from home.'

'What about school?'

'Reckon I've just about finished with school.'

'What about the cricket game?'

'Reckon I've just about finished with cricket, too.'

Robbo was appalled by this heresy, but his friendship prompted him to think of other things.

'Where are you staying? Have you got somewhere to sleep?'

'Yeah,' said Joe, strangely comforted by the thought of the culvert and the down-and-out. 'I've got a doss to go back to.'

But there was still another harsh lesson Joe had to learn about the ways of the world. When he collected his papers and went along to the street pitch, he found it already occupied. The bigger boy who had bashed him up on his first day was there shouting the headline news:

'Pye-up! Pye-up! Japanese offensive in Manchuria. Pye-up!'

The bigger boy was showing signs of wear and tear and had a thoroughly belligerent air about him. The picture was clear enough. Someone had muscled in on the bigger boy's pitch – and he'd moved down onto Joe's.

Oh, God no, he thought. It wasn't going to happen all over again, was it? He swallowed hard and moved uncertainly forward. 'What are you doing on my pitch?' Joe demanded, trying to sound as tough as he could.

The interloper ignored him and kept crying: 'Pye-up! Pye-up! Atrocities in Manchuria . . .'

'You get off my pitch,' cried Joe, but the bigger boy turned with a savage snarl and brandished a very big, hard and grubby, clenched fist.

'Ain't yours any more!' he snarled. '*My* stand now, and if you don't get out of the way, mug, I'll bash your brains out.'

The ferocity of the other boy's response thoroughly intimidated Joe. He couldn't really win this one, could he? The only thing left to do, it seemed, was to play the game according to the rules.

The little paper boy had found a pitch near the viaduct down round the corner. In his jaunty, cocksparrow way he was making the best of it and had invented a variation of his own on the traditional cry.

'Pye-*er*-up! Bradman's health in doubt. Big battle in Manchuria. Pye-er-*up*! Reedawlabartit!'

The call was cut off abruptly as he saw Joe advancing towards him. He stood there, wary and alarmed.

'Come on, git out of it,' said Joe roughly. 'This stand's mine now.' He felt deeply ashamed but resolute. What other choice did he have? Big fish eat little fish.

'Come on, beat it, you little mongrel,' he said, doing his best snarl with the same ferocity that the big standover kid had used to intimidate him.

But the smaller boy proved as valiant as before. He dropped his papers and came on with his arms flailing. Joe grabbed the small fists and held tight, for all the other boy's struggling. And then, alarmingly, despite himself he started to cry. He shook the smaller boy frantically and with tears streaming down his face shouted at him:

'Just get out! Don't make me hit you. For God's sake, just get out of it!'

The other boy was both puzzled and shocked by what he saw as Joe's totally inexplicable behaviour.

'All right,' he said, 'I'll go. What the hell are

you crying about? It's me that's being given the bum's rush. It's a rotten world.'

As Joe stood in possession of the pitch under the viaduct he tried out the new call he'd heard the smaller boy using.

'Pye-*er*-up Reedawlabartit! Pye-er-*up*!'

But his heart wasn't in it. The kid was right, it really was a pretty rotten world.

He felt oddly comforted when he returned to the park after finishing selling that evening and found his down-and-out mate of the night before there to greet him. He made him welcome at the fire he'd got going in a small metal drum with holes punched round the sides.

The down-and-out, whose name turned out to be Harry, seemed equally pleased to see him. He'd scrounged some tea and sugar and had a brew going in an old black billy set on the fire. Joe watched with admiration as he tossed the tea leaves into the seething water and swung the billy round a couple of times in a full circle.

'Settles the leaves,' explained Harry. Then he added approvingly: 'See you've brought along some papers to keep you warm tonight.'

'Yeah,' said Joe. 'Brought a little bit of tucker for us, too.'

As they sat round the dying fire in the darkness of the night, Harry's face in the ember-glow was ravaged and thoughtful.

'You know, Joe,' he said, 'I been thinking about things and I've come to the conclusion that the earth is actually Hell.'

'You reckon?' said Joe. It was a field of speculation that had never occurred to him before.

'Yeah, I do,' said Harry. 'I reckon this is Hell, where we're being punished for what we did before.'

'Before *when*?' asked Joe, who had a practical sort of mind.

'In a previous life, of course,' said Harry. 'You've heard about reincarnation. I reckon what's happening now is punishment for what we done when we lived before.'

Joe looked round at their miserable abode. 'Jeez,' he said, after a moment's thought. 'If that's so, we must have been real bad when we lived last time.'

Harry cackled at a sudden thought. 'I just hope we enjoyed ourselves while we were being stinkers,' he said – and Joe could not help grinning at him. 'Want another cuppa?'

'Yeah. Ta,' said Joe. A bit shyly he produced a small paper bag from his pocket. 'I bought these for us for a sort of a treat.'

'Raisins!' Harry was delighted. 'Good on you, mate. All them vitamins. Keep you from getting scurvy, y'know.' He munched the dried fruit appreciatively. 'You're a good mate, Joe. Good mates are better'n gold.'

The thought warmed Joe as he went to sleep under the culvert – after discovering that the

44

experts were right and newspapers padded under your clothes did keep you warm against the chill night air.

Most of your body anyway.

CHAPTER 6

When Joe woke next morning he realized there was something different in the atmosphere. At first he couldn't place what it might be. He huddled in his makeshift bed and thought about it in a vague way.

Couldn't put his finger on it . . . Then suddenly he heard the church bells ringing. Of course, that was it! It was Sunday, and even at this hour of the morning the sounds and rhythms of the city were quite different to any other day of the week. There was none of that feeling of stirring and restlessness that comes with a great city preparing for the day's work.

'Ready for a cuppa, mate?' asked Harry, carefully lifting the black billy up from where it was keeping warm on the bed of coals.

'Yeah, ta,' said Joe. 'Reckon it was my turn to make it, really.'

'Ah, I let you sleep in a bit on account of it being Sunday. Like it says in the Bible: Six days shalt thou labour and the seventh day shalt thou rest.'

Joe took his mug of tea thoughtfully. It was all very well for the Bible to say that, but with the single-minded purpose that was driving him, he wasn't looking forward to a day of rest at all. All it meant to him was a wasted day. With no morning paper round and no street sales, it was the one day of the week he wasn't going to make a bob at all.

But when he mentioned this drawback, Harry was cheerful about it. Possibly on the basis that it was easier to be philosophical about someone else's problems, he urged Joe to bear in mind the old saying about all work and no play.

'Tell you what, mate,' he said. 'What say we take a stroll downtown to look at the sights. Then we'll have lunch at a pretty special restaurant I know. And after that we'll go down the Domain and see the fun there.'

'Aw knock it off, Harry,' said Joe. 'You know we haven't got any money to go round eating in restaurants.'

Harry laid a finger along his nose, looking cunning and gleeful.

'That's what's real special about this place,' he chuckled. 'You don't need money to eat there.'

'Then they'll want something else,' said Joe with a conviction born out of his recent experiences. 'No one gives you anything for free.'

'Well, you do have to go along to the service first,' admitted Harry. 'But that's no hardship, is it? All they do is a bit of praying and sing a few hymns. Nothing like a good hymn to give a bloke an appetite.'

For lack of any information to the contrary, Joe was prepared to agree, but he had the sort of mind that liked to follow through an idea once he got hold of it.

'Do you reckon it's exactly honest to go along and pretend you're religious just to get a feed?'

'Well, now look, Joe, I don't think that's quite the way to look at it,' said Harry happily, with the tone of a man who was prepared to look at all sides in any discussion. 'If you go into a hash house and get a meal, you pay for it with money, don't you?'

'Yeah,' agreed Joe. 'Or if you don't, they call the cops.'

Harry ignored this as being a bit frivolous and getting away from the point.

'But in this case I'm talking about, you pay for your meal by getting preached at a bit and joining in the singing. What's the difference, really? In both cases you pay your way, don't you?'

Joe was dubious, but Harry warmed to his theme.

'You see, mate, it's a matter of supply and demand. *They* need a congregation and *you* need a feed. And don't you worry about deceiving them because you're not really being religious, or because you're only moving your lips and pretending you know the words.'

'No, they don't want pious people, what they want's a sinner. So you're just giving them what they want, aren't you? Supply and demand. And what you want's a feed. They've got it there and want to give it to you. How do you think they'd feel if they took the trouble to cook all that tucker and nobody came along to eat it?'

'But it's charity, isn't it?' said Joe doubtfully. He'd been brought up in the vague understanding that to accept charity was a shameful thing. And there was another phrase he'd heard his father use often enough, 'It's the principle of the thing.'

'Tell you what, mate,' said Harry, 'when you're really hungry and someone offers you a feed, it's hard to hang on to a principle like that.'

When they finished their breakfast (which consisted of a tin mug full of strong, sweet black tea – and then another one) they assembled their belongings, folded the old newspapers that served as blankets and tucked them safely away up under the beams of the culvert, and set out on what Harry had optimistically described as 'a stroll downtown to see the sights'.

Their path led them a little way across the city and past Central railway station. It was not all that far to the Riordan home, but though Joe kept a wary eye out he saw none of the family, nor any of the neighbours he knew.

They walked through the park in front of the station and up the hill past the famous Tivoli theatre – though no one ever called it that. 'The Tiv' was how it was universally known.

'Wouldn't mind going to the old Tiv,' said Harry. 'Just what a bloke needs in times like these. You ever see Stiffy and Mo?'

Joe shook his head. Though of course he'd *heard* about them. Everyone knew Mo's famous catch-cries, like 'Strike me lucky!' and 'Suck it and see!'

'Talk about funny!' said Harry. 'Funniest act there ever was on a stage, anywhere, those two.'

A few blocks further up they came to Hyde Park. In the first section of it work was under way for the building of the grand memorial for the dead of the 1914-18 war. The war that ended about the time that Joe was born.

At the other end of the park, work was nearing completion on the fountain with great bronze figures which Mr Archibald was having built as a tribute to the city. Across from it was the imposing bulk of the Cathedral and beyond this, but out of sight, was the great open space of the Domain, where Harry had suggested they should go later 'to see the fun'.

Harry rattled on about the things they passed. It was funny, thought Joe, he'd lived here all his life, but Harry, who was really a bushie, knew more about the town than he did. Maybe a visitor always saw more than people who lived in a place all the time.

Joe had always been respectfully aware of the tall buildings in the heart of the city. But until Harry told him he hadn't realized that some of them were actually more than 150 feet high!

Skyscrapers they called them. Maybe people were right when they claimed it was madness to try to build any higher. Of course they weren't nearly as high as the ones they built in New York. But an unbelievable lot of mad things went on in America.

There was plenty of traffic in the streets by this time; cars parked along the kerbs and taxi-cabs plying the streets looking for fares. They admired and criticized the new models, and Harry had plenty to say about what sort of car he'd buy when he struck it rich.

Which was looking, perhaps, a long way into the future, since they were walking (as were many others in the city that morning). They did not care to spend, or did not have, the few pence it would have cost to ride on the rattling tram cars that would have taken them down to Circular Quay in a few minutes.

Harry and Joe spent a good deal of time pleasurably peering into shop-windows at displays of the latest fashions. Harry, though very funny at the expense of some of the things ladies were expected to wear that season, was rather taken with some of the men's clobber that was on display. He particularly fancied a wide-brimmed felt hat in the window of David Jones' store.

'How do you reckon I'd look in that, mate?' he demanded, standing back to eye the model, and, meanwhile, adjusting his own battered hat to the same rakish angle as that in the window.

51

'You'd look like a real toff,' Joe assured him. 'Like a rich squatter.'

It was a time when every man wore a hat. Anyone going bareheaded would stick out in the street as something of an oddity. Joe himself had not yet graduated beyond the peaked cap which was the traditional headwear for boys, and many workingmen. Privately he tried to imagine how he would look in a new felt hat. If things came good he might even get it – one day. But one with a narrower brim, he thought, than the one Harry was admiring in the window.

They made their way down near the Quay, where Harry led Joe to a small hall in one of the back streets. They were welcomed in as 'brothers' and the uniformed doorkeeper handed them each a small and grimy numbered card.

'Don't lose it,' Harry muttered to Joe out of the corner of his mouth. 'That's for the tucker later.'

There were about thirty other men in the hall in similar situation to themselves. All bore the unmistakeable signs of being down on their luck. Most of them were subdued, selfconscious and a little ill at ease.

But when it came to the point, Joe found that being prayed over wasn't that bad after all. The brass band with the big drum was rousing, and he was sure the girl with the tambourine was the same one he had admired when he'd watched the Sallies at their street meeting while he was on his pitch. She was great. She could really handle a tambourine!

Joe felt a sudden pang of misery when the major who was leading the service spoke of the coming Christmas season; but, to his surprise, he enjoyed joining in the hymns – lah-lahing along energetically, even when he wasn't certain of the words. And when he recognized the chorus he had heard before, he joined in with great gusto . . .

Bread of Heaven,
Bread of Heaven,
Feed me till I want no more . . .

And that was pretty much what they did when the gospel meeting was over and they set up the trestle tables and served the meal. Thick barley broth soup, rather tough roast mutton with sticky brown gravy and mounds of cabbage and mashed potato.

Joe hadn't realized, until the food was on the table in front of him, just how hungry he was. Harry was right, he thought fleetingly. This was no time to be worried about principles.

He hoed into the meal and, following the example of his fellow diners, cleaned his plate with the crust of the thick hand of bread that had accompanied it. Harry gave him a wink as he slipped a slice inside his jacket. 'Take a hunk of dodger for later,' he whispered.

The meal ended splendidly with a dollop of bread and butter pudding with a ladle of thin custard over it. And the whole lot washed down with a big mug of strong, sweet tea with milk in it. Joe reckoned he couldn't have eaten another mouthful – and that it was about as great a meal as he'd ever had in his life. The Sallies were pretty wonderful.

When the meal was over, most of the men dispersed, going their ways singly or in pairs. Many of them still had that subdued selfconscious air – as though they felt guilty, or apologetic.

But a small group, Harry and Joe among them, strolled to the waterfront and sat together on the piles and beams at the edge of the wharf. They watched the ferries churning across the harbour and gliding in and out of their berths at the Quay. Hundreds of small craft were busy tacking to and fro on the sparkling blue water. And dominating it all, of course, was the great arch of The Bridge, recently finished and still a matter of awe and wonder to the inhabitants of the city.

Harry was happily puffing away at a stubby foul-smelling pipe. The other men sat smoking, too, one of them expressing the popular opinion that there was nothing quite like a smoke after a good tuck-in like they'd had.

It was perhaps the memory of the meal that prompted the oldest of the group, a spry, little man with a wrinkled and leathery face, to offer rare hospitality to Joe.

'Would you like a fag, young'n?' he offered expansively. 'Have a go at the makings.'

'I don't smoke,' said Joe, a bit embarrassed. 'I never got a taste for it.'

'And you stay that way too, mate,' Harry urged. 'You're better off without it. I just wish I'd never taken it up myself.' Though the relish with which he sucked on the reeking pipe seemed to belie the words.

An argument began with some for and some against what was sometimes fancifully referred to as The Lady Nicotine. Some, while puffing away themselves, joined with Harry in urging Joe never to take up the filthy habit. Others assured him that there was no harm at all in it and that God knew a man needed some sort of solace in times such as they were going through.

The old man who had offered Joe the makings of a cigarette in the first place was loudest in his defence of the weed. He'd read opinions from doctors – not just ordinary doctors, but *specialists* – who reckoned that smoking was actually beneficial. And apart from that he was prepared to take the evidence of his old granny who'd smoked a pipe continuously every day of her life and was fit as a trout right up to the day she died at ninety-seven.

Having advised Joe for and against smoking, the group somehow got round to discussing what was the best thing for a young fellow like him to do in the hard times they were going through. They argued mainly whether he was better off battling in the city or the bush, and opinion was about as equally divided on this as it had been on the question of nicotine.

Some reckoned that the bush was the only place, (though it might have been pointed out that they themselves were not in it) and others maintained stoutly that there was better chance of surviving in the town.

The leathery little man, who seemed to be the ultimate authority, declared that the bush *had* been the place for a battler, but not any more. There was a time, he said, when a bloke on the track had only to appear at the kitchen door of any farm or station to be given the traditional handout – ten, ten, two and a quarter. Ten pounds weight of flour, that was, with another ten pounds of meat, two of sugar and quarter of tea.

But not any more, the little man said. There were altogether too many blokes on the track these days. The bush was ruined for the battler, just as the town was.

CHAPTER 7

Harry had seemed unnaturally quiet during the waterfront discussion on the relative virtues of Sydney or the Bush, and, as they trudged up the hill on their way to the Domain, Joe sounded him out on it.

'What d'you reckon, then?'

'I reckon a working man can't win these days, wherever he might be,' said Harry gloomily.

As they topped the rise and walked down into the great open expanse, Harry seemed to recover something of his earlier spirits. And he was delighted with Joe's reaction to the colourful scene he was introducing him to.

It was a fine and sunny afternoon and the populace had flocked to the Domain – or 'The Dom', as it was popularly referred to – not just because it was the cheapest (being free) but also because it was far and away the best entertainment offering anywhere in the city. The whole landscape was crowded with people – parading along the paths, picnicking under the shade of the trees, and gathered in groups to appreciate the highlight of the carnival . . . the soapbox orators.

'You never seen this before?' asked Harry.

'Mean to say you've been living here in the city all your life and you never been to Speakers' Corner in The Dom on a Sunday afternoon?'

'Never,' said Joe in wonderment. 'What are all those blokes standing up there talking about?'

'Anything you like to mention,' said Harry. 'You name it and one or other of those blokes is likely to be talking about it. Anyone at all can bring along a soapbox and stand up here and say his piece. You can criticize the premier or the prime minister or the king – even God. You can say anything you like – and anyone can disagree with you if *they* like.'

Joe thought about it.

'Sounds fair enough.'

'It's what you call Democracy and The Right of Free Speech.' Harry made the declaration with considerable pride, almost as though he'd had a hand in the arrangement of it.

'Let's go and see what they're on about,' said Joe.

There was a variety of fashion in the rostrums from which the speeches were being delivered. Some spoke from assembled platforms with flags or banners waving overhead, others, in the true spirit, carried their soapboxes with them – and set them down and mounted them wherever an audience seemed likely.

The various speakers tended to set themselves up far enough apart so as to ensure a certain privacy for their own particular crowd. Sometimes these overlapped by design because the main sport came from the duel of wit and insult between the rival orators. Each speaker would pour scorn and derision on his opponent's arguments and beg the audience to bear witness to the other's illogic and intemperance and stupidity.

The crowds loved this sort of exchange and would egg them on, goading each speaker in turn and loudly applauding the most barbed thrust and the wild excess of vituperation.

A bit removed from all the raucous voices, a brass band was giving a concert recital to a more sedate audience, and further along from them the Sallies had seized the opportunity to set up a gospel meeting. On the fringes of the crowds in Speakers' Corner there were maybe a dozen itinerant musicians. Each had a hat hopefully upturned at his feet and pathetically few coins lying in it as bait.

One was the very image of the traditional swaggie. His trouser legs were tied below the knee with bowyangs. He carried a bluey over his shoulder, with a black billy dangling from it. An old kelpie dog crouched beside him, its head resting on its forepaws and its bright eyes watching the passing crowd. The hat upturned on the ground in front of him had corks tied with string to its brim. Joe noted that he seemed to be getting more than his share of what little money was going. The old swaggie busker was playing on the traditional bush instrument – a gum leaf – and the tune was the sentimental old Irish ballad, 'Danny Boy'.

Some of the speakers obviously had their own loyal following of people who came to listen to them alone, but mostly the crowd drifted from one to another . . . listening for a moment to what each was saying before passing on. Or else they might get caught up in an argument, or heckling, to their liking and stay to listen or join in. Sometimes they heckled in their own right, or took issue with those who did so and started arguments of their own on the side.

As they did the rounds it seemed to Joe that Harry was right when he said that anything you could think of might be being talked about. There were speakers in favour of God and speakers against God. Others wanted to persuade their fellow citizens to take up vegetarianism, or give up alcohol or tobacco or wear loose clothing and take cold seawater baths and go barefoot.

One bloke who particularly took Joe's fancy had a high singsong voice and long white hair and preached the message that the earth was flat. He declared that all the troubles and miseries of society stemmed from the human race not understanding this simple fact. Listening to the fervent flow of reasoning, Joe felt himself beginning to waver. There seemed to be a mad sort of logic to the whole thing.

Logic of various degrees of madness was the theme for the main body of speakers under the banners of a dozen or more political parties and philosophies, most of which Joe had never even heard. But each of them had a different cure for the scourge of unemployment and misery resulting from the Great Depression; and each had someone, or something, different to blame as the cause of it.

The Communist Party, with its red flag and hammer and sickle emblem, had one of the largest and rowdiest of the crowds. Standing on the edge of it, Joe saw Jack up on the platform beside the speaker, and Jack, catching his eye, gave him a quick clenched-fist salute.

It was towards the end of the afternoon, when the shadows were lengthening and people beginning to drift away, that the disturbing thing happened.

Joe had lost track of Harry in the crowd, and, when he caught up, found him listening intently to a woman who was addressing a small group on the outskirts. She had no flag or banner and he never did find out who she was speaking for.

She was different from most of the others. She spoke simply and conversationally – having nothing of the stentorian bellow cultivated by most street orators to make their voices carry in the open air. Yet every word she spoke came over clearly.

As he approached she was apparently ending her speech, and saying, 'That's what I want you to bear in mind, friends. It's a terrible thing to see men tramping the streets, willing to work and unable to find work. Hungry and defeated men sitting in parks and sleeping in alleyways. But when you see these men I want you to think not only of them but of the women and children you do not see. The starving and homeless and desperate women and children who these would be supporting if only they had the work which surely to God they are entitled to.'

Joe was caught by the sincerity in the woman's voice, and the words she said. And when he looked at Harry he saw that his eyes were brimming with tears.

'You all right, mate?' he asked, with something like alarm.

Harry turned his head away rather too quickly.

'Yeah, I'm fine,' he said gruffly. 'Guess we'd better be getting back.'

They walked back across the city to their park in silence; not really an uncomfortable silence, but as though each of them was deep in his own thoughts.

As they kindled the fire for the billy and laid out the thick wedges of bread they had souvenired for their supper, Joe said, 'Thanks for taking me there today. I reckon I learned a lot.'

'That's all right, mate,' said Harry. 'Reckon I learned a lot myself today.'

As Joe adjusted the paper insulation inside his clothes and composed himself for sleep, he realized that Harry's cough, which he hadn't noticed all day, was troubling him again. And he seemed to have lost all his spirit.

He had no idea how long he had slept, and could not at first work out what it was that had woken him. Then he heard Harry's hacking cough, and the even more distressing sound of deep convulsive sobbing. The fire in the iron drum had died down to leave only the faintest glow, and he could just make out Harry's silhouette.

The older man was crouched with his arms folded as though hugging his chest, and trying to protect it from the harsh tubercular coughing which racked him. At the same time he was weeping bitterly, but seemed to be trying both to cough and sob quietly so as not to disturb his young mate.

Joe felt a deep distress. His instinct was to speak – to try to comfort Harry – but he knew he had no words that would really help in this situation.

63

He must have fallen asleep as he lay there miserably concluding that there was nothing he could do to help. The next thing he was aware of was the morning sun striking in.

Harry was up before him, making his cursory ablutions at the water bubbler, what Joe's mum called a lick and a promise. But there was something different about him this morning. His face was clearer, his expression not quite as defeated as it had been. There was a look of new purpose about him – as though he had come to a decision.

He'd already stoked the fire and boiled the billy.

'Have a cuppa, mate,' he said, seeing Joe awake. 'I'm gonna hit the track early. I did a lot of thinking last night and I came to the conclusion that this is no good. No flamin' good at all!'

He was gathering up his few possessions as he spoke and packing them into a swag.

'Where are you off to then?' asked Joe. He felt downcast, and a sense of loss.

'Going back up the bush, mate,' said Harry with determination. 'Back up the bush where I should never have left. Gotta get things sorted out. Gotta talk things over and get it all straightened out.'

'Who with?'

'With me wife, mate. With me wife and little boy. I been a bloody mug, and that's a fact. But maybe it's not too late.'

Harry swung his swag on his shoulder and glanced round to make sure he hadn't left anything behind.

'Been good to know you, Joe,' he said.

They shook hands firmly.

'You too,' said Joe.

'You been a good mate,' said Harry. 'Look after yourself.'

'Yeah,' said Joe. 'You too.'

He felt a pang of loneliness as he watched the shabby figure of his friend go. Harry paused a little way along the path as he was shaken by one of his coughing fits. He turned and waved once . . . then he trudged round the corner and was lost from sight.

Joe was early at the loading bays to collect his papers for the street sales. He sat on the hard wooden bench outside O'Brien's cluttered little office. Brooding to himself – he had a lot to think about.

O'Brien had seen a lot of kids come and go in his business. He knew some of the problems they might be facing, particularly in times like these. He could recognize certain signs.

'Hey, Joe,' he said. 'If you want to wash up there's a shower just along the back there.'

'Yeah,' said Joe cautiously.

'No trouble if you want to use it,' O'Brien assured him.

Joe was embarrassed. 'Is there a towel?'

O'Brien grinned at him. 'Well, sort of. You'll have to improvise, like they used to say in the army.'

The washroom was draughty, but the water was hot and felt wonderfully good. And Joe found out what improvisation meant when it came to drying himself on sheets of newsprint that had been cut to small-towel size. There was a thick wad of them, with a hole punched through the corner, hung on a loop of wire from a nail near the shower stall.

It took a lot of them to dry a boy Joe's size. There always seemed to be one wet clammy bit left, the small of the back being particularly difficult to dry.

But it felt much better afterwards, and seemed to clarify Joe's thoughts and determine him on a course of action. He'd been a mug, too, hadn't he? And there was something he had to do about it.

Very cautiously he approached the corner where he had previously had his stand. Yes. The big lout who had bashed him up at his first pitch, and then driven him away from this one, was still there hawking his papers.

'Pye-up! Pye-up! Globetrotter shot. Murder on yacht. Pye-up!'

With his breath coming more quickly than

usual, Joe sized his antagonist up. Well, he wasn't *that* much bigger than he was. And everyone reckoned that if you just hit back at a bully hard enough he'd show yellow.

Joe laid his papers down and came up stealthily behind. He tapped him on the shoulder, and as the bigger kid turned he sent up a quick prayer – and hit him as hard as he could. Then, in desperation and out of anger for all the injustices he had suffered, he just kept hitting and hitting.

His opponent tried to fight back but the suddenness and savagery of the attack had demoralized him. In a few moments he was blubbing and terrified. Crying quits and pleading – all right, all right, there was no need to try and kill him.

'Well, just get going,' roared Joe, breathless and triumphant. 'This is *my* pitch. Just get out of here and don't come back or a lot worse'll happen to you.'

The other boy scurried away and waited till he was well out of reach before turning with a snivelling threat, 'You ain't heard the last of this.'

'Get out,' snarled Joe. 'Or I'll give you some more.' Then, as he noticed the way the other boy was heading, he warned him: 'And lay off that other kid down the next corner. You try and muscle in on his pitch and I'll do more than half kill you.'

It was a pretty rotten way to live he supposed,

but if that was the way they played the game he had no choice, did he?

'Pye-*er*-up! Gruesome murder. Pye-er-*up*!'

He was glad he'd thought of the little kid down on the next corner.

CHAPTER 8

When Mr O'Brien handed over his pay envelope it had 18/6d pencilled against his name. Eighteen shillings and sixpence!

'How does that compare with others?' Joe asked.

'Good,' said the big, beefy man encouragingly. 'For your second week that's quite good.'

That night, standing at the edge of the light from the street lamp outside the row of tenements that included the Riordan house, Joe made a painful appraisal. He took two florins out of the pay envelope. Then, after further calculation, another shilling.

He licked the flap of the envelope closed again – though it didn't stick very well – and, with a stub of pencil he'd acquired, scrawled on the flap: 'Mrs Elsie Riordan. Personal and Private.'

Softfooted he approached the house and slipped the envelope through the letterbox in the door. It fell with a distinct clunk on the floor inside and he heard his mother's voice, 'What's that? Who's there?'

He took to his heels.

Standing in the lighted doorway with the envelope in her hand Mrs Riordan called, 'Joe. Joe. Don't run away!'

But by that time there was neither sight nor sound of him.

In a turmoil of emotion from his hit and run visit to home, Joe trudged through lamplit streets with their dark-shadowed doorways and alleys. And when at last he began to tire he turned automatically towards the park and the culvert where he had stayed with Harry.

But when he got near he saw that the hide-away was already occupied by dark figures, and a bottle was passing hand to hand among them. Joe hesitated, but could not bring himself to try to join their company.

He walked a long while through the streets, until, just as his need for sleep was becoming really desperate – almost as though directed by fate – he found himself outside an entrance over which a big, shabby sign proclaimed: People's Palace. A refuge for those who were not quite so down-and-out as to be completely broke.

The man at the desk behind the barred window was wearily benevolent. 'Yes, we've still got a bed going.'

'How much is it?' asked Joe cautiously.

'As much as you can afford,' said the man at

the window. He looked Joe up and down sympathetically. 'Could you manage sixpence?'

'Yeah, reckon I could afford a zac.'

Well, a bloke was entitled to make a bit of a splash on payday, wasn't he?

The big dormitory room was dingy, the mattress lumpy and the blankets thin. The lights were put out early, but you could still make out the rows of beds and the figures in them in the reflection from the corridors outside.

The man in the next bed had a soft, persistent cough and others groaned or muttered or ground their teeth and cried out in their sleep.

In the middle of the night Joe woke to the sound of someone sobbing, not loudly but persistently in a heartbroken way. For a moment he thought it was Harry and he was back under the culvert in the park again. Then he became aware of the figure sitting on the edge of the bed nearby. The man held his head in his hands and was weeping quietly and hopelessly.

'Aw shut up!' someone cried from one of the other beds. 'Stow it for God's sake, mate. Let other people get some sleep.'

The weeper fell silent. Joe saw him crawl back under the blankets and could hear the man, still, sniffling and gulping quietly to himself.

Everyone was woken right on dawn at the Palace and got up grumbling and coughing and cursing in muttered undertones. Joe washed and dressed quickly. He was glad enough of the mug of sweet tea and thick slice of bread and jam they offered for breakfast, but was also glad enough to be out of the place.

As he walked briskly up into the steep little streets of Surry Hills to do his paper round he thought that in many ways, the culvert in the park and Harry's billy tea and the fire burning in the little iron drum had been better than the dormitory.

And he'd had to pay for the Palace, what's more! Sixpence a night. He really couldn't afford to waste money like that – just for somewhere to sleep.

That afternoon, as he hawked his papers on the corner, he looked up and saw his mother coming along the street towards him. Of course he'd known that she could find him if she put her mind to it. Nothing to do but wait for her.

'How are you, Joe?' she asked. Her voice was calm and quiet, but he knew what an effort it was for her to keep it normal.

'I'm fine, Mum. Not to worry. I'm fine.'

'Come home, Joe.'

'Not while *he's* there,' he declared stubbornly.

'Don't blame your dad, love,' she begged him.

'After what he did? Someone's got to be blamed. And he did take the money and spend it on booze.'

'And that's something I want to see you about, too, Joe.' She held out the small pay envelope he had dropped through the letterbox the night before. 'I can't take this from you. Not if you're not at home. You've got to live too, son.'

'I took some,' said Joe. 'I've got enough to get by.'

His mother smiled proudly but sadly at him.

'You're a good boy, but don't try to tell me that. I know how much it costs to live. Just come home.'

'Not while *he's* there,' Joe insisted.

There was a pause. Then his mother said very gently, 'I know how you feel, but your father's a good man really, Joe. What's happened to him – getting the sack and all that – is the worst thing that ever happened to him in his life. But he really is sorry for what happened between you and him.'

There was another pause. Then his mother pleaded, 'Come home at least for Christmas day.'

Joe looked down a bit shamefaced. 'Yeah. Well, all right then.'

His mother still stood there, dignified and calm. Without trying to touch him she said, 'I love you, Joe.'

He did not dare to look up. 'You too, Mum. See you Christmas day.'

He watched her walk away down the street. And when he began to chant the newsboy cry

73

again, the words choked in his throat for a moment.

Over the next couple of weeks he settled down to a routine. The morning round and street selling occupied most of his days. Late evening and Sunday he often saw Jack and sometimes attended meetings.

Mostly he slept out of doors – 'sleeping rough' as they called it. Not only did he begrudge the money, but the dormitory, with its feeling of being confined behind locked doors and men who moaned or groaned in their sleep, was little more comforting than a makeshift shelter out of doors.

It was at the Palace, another night, that he suffered a hard loss and learned another bitter lesson. Waking, the first thing he did, as usual, was to check the few shillings in his shirt pocket – only to find the money gone.

He couldn't believe it at first, but it was gone all right. One of the men – seeing Joe frantically searching his pockets – asked what was the matter.

When Joe told him he was sympathetic in a brutal sort of way.

'Well, that's the way it goes. You gotta watch it all the time, kid. Steal your back teeth, this lot, unless you keep your mouth shut.'

It had only been a couple of shillings, but it

was two days before payday and it meant a hard and hungry forty-eight hours for Joe. It was a lesson he never forgot. Sleeping rough, he learned how to guard his money and his clothes. Boots in particular. You had to watch your boots, or they'd have them away from you.

CHAPTER 9

Fortunately it was building up to real Christmas weather, with hot days and warm nights, and sleeping out was not such a terrible hardship. He worked hard and seemed to be doing better day by day. At the end of the week he felt entitled to take a few extra bob out for himself.

One night, as he surreptitiously slipped the pay envelope through the letterbox, the door opened suddenly and his father was standing there.

'Come inside,' he begged. 'Joe, I want to talk to you. Please come inside.'

Joe backed hastily away.

'We got nothing to talk about,' he said in a harsh tone. He turned on his heel and strode quickly into the darkness, ignoring his father's pleading voice behind him. 'Joe, Joe. Come back!'

The signs of Christmas were all around. There were decorations in shop windows and some people had put Christmas wreaths or sprigs of imitation holly or greenery of some sort on their doors. In the big stores, musicians at portable organs, or wind-up gramophones with large trumpet-shaped speakers, were playing hymns and carols.

Christmas was the theme from all the radio stations, too, and the Sallies were out in strength – the brass bands playing and the big drums beating – to preach the Christmas message.

But Jack mounted his soapbox to proclaim a seasonal message of a somewhat different kind.

'Christmas is the opiate of the people. It is their way of trying to convince you that things are not quite as bad as you know very well they are. Christmas is the exception that should prove the rule. The one good day that shows how things should be on every day, but never are.

'This should be our way of life . . . Generous, loving, communal and prosperous. Good food on the table and good wishes at the end of the day . . . on *every* table, comrades, and at the end of *every* day. It's a season of goodwill which should be for everyone and for all the year. It's the way things should be, comrades, but never are!'

Of course, they hadn't stopped to listen to him; not even the deadbeats and down-and-outs.

'I dunno,' said Jack in disgust. 'No one seems to care.'

'You said a lot of true things in there, Jack,'
said Joe.

Jack was grateful for that. 'Thanks, comrade.
Come round the hall and have a cuppa tea.'

Joe excused himself. 'Something I've gotta
do.'

What he had to do entailed serious discussion with the man in the bootshop. He was a
little, baldheaded pixie sort of man who wore a
leather apron and worked over his cobbler's
last, peering through thick-lensed glasses.

He listened to Joe's ideas sympathetically.

'Yes,' he said, 'I reckon it'd work at that.' He
put the tins of Kiwi boot polish on the counter.
'You'll need one brown and one black, of
course. That'll set you back two bob. But you'll
get fifty shines or more out of these big tins.
And these brushes . . . they're a bit second-
hand . . . reckon you can have them for two
bob, too.'

Joe was a bit awed by the size of his capital
investment, but realized he was getting a
bargain.

'Yeah, well thanks. And you wouldn't have
any rags, like, would you? Reckon I'll need
them for polishing.'

The bootmaker looked at him speculatively.
'Well look, young fella, I got rags here that are
just going to waste. I'll throw them in for

nothing – on account of you being a good cus-
tomer and just starting up in business for
yourself.'

So Joe added a new call to his repertoire.
'Shine. Shoe shine, mister. See you face in'm
for a trey.' There was not exactly a roaring trade
in this line of business, but at threepence a time
it was pretty well clear profit. Just for a smear of
polish and lashings of elbow grease.

With the morning round for Jack Crabtree,
and selling on the street for Mr O'Brien, and
with a bit extra coming in from the shoeshine
business, he calculated he was enabling the
family to hold its own.

Then, almost before he realized it, it was the
day before Christmas. Christmas Eve, and
everywhere they seemed to be playing the carol
about how away in the manger, no crib for his
bed, the little Lord Jesus laid down his sweet
head . . .

Joe reckoned he knew just how the little Lord
Jesus must have felt about that – he was in
much the same position.

When he went to collect his money from
O'Brien there was a small surprise. First the pay
packet – twenty-one shillings and fourpence.
His best week yet. And apart from that there
was a Christmas card in the envelope. Just a
perfunctory 'Season's Greetings' with a few

bells and holly branches printed around it – but a Christmas card nonetheless.

'Merry Christmas, Joe,' said Mr O'Brien as he saw him standing there with the card in his hand.

'Thanks, Mr O'Brien,' said Joe. 'Merry Christmas to you, too.'

As he was leaving the big, beefy man called after him. 'Joe!'

He turned round. 'Yeah, Mr O'Brien?'

'And a happy New Year.'

It was a fine mild night and small groups of people were singing in the parks, *Oh come all ye faithful, joyful and triumphant* . . . He found himself drawn back to the place where he had spent the first homeless night. He wondered if Harry had succeeded in making it back up the bush, and whether he'd straightened things out with his wife and kid.

There were three down-and-outs already under the culvert, but, perhaps in the spirit of the season, they welcomed Joe among them. In this light they couldn't see how young he was, or maybe it didn't matter any more.

'Come and park yourself down here, mate,' said one. 'Plenty of room at this inn,' said another. 'Merry Christmas,' said the third.

They passed round a bottle, and Joe took a small experimental sip in his turn. He made appreciative noises, but privately he thought it tasted lousy. Sweet but fiery, and sort of sickly. Not wanting to be impolite, he raised the bottle to his lips the next time, but didn't drink.

On an impulse he passed round the bag of raisins he'd been hanging onto for a breakfast treat – or maybe even to take home.

He didn't have anything much to take home, and that had been another painful decision. He'd decided that the money he had was too important to be spent on gifts, the way things were.

Though there'd been one present he *had* to buy.

Joe woke with the sun next morning, had a quick lick and promise at the bubbler, gathered up his things and was on his way. Only to realize that he was too early. They probably wouldn't even be up yet.

He walked halfway down into the city then back round Central railway station. His step got slower and slower as he climbed the steep path into Surry Hills and approached the front door of the house that had become alien to him.

The door swung open even before he had finished knocking, and his mother was there with a look of delight on her face. 'Oh Joe!' She took him in her arms.

He kissed her. 'Merry Christmas, Mum!' In another moment his brothers and sisters all were there, laughing and shouting and thumping him playfully or hugging him.

His father had been standing back and as they dragged Joe into the room, father and son came face to face. There was silence as they regarded one another steadily for a moment.

'Happy Christmas, son,' said John Riordan.

'Yeah,' said Joe. 'Happy Christmas, Dad.'

It wasn't the most sumptuous of festive dinners – featuring the leg of mutton in place of the leg of ham, and emphasizing the virtues of baked rabbit rather than the roast goose or turkey. But it was merry enough in its way.

Joe and his father behaved to one another with studied courtesy. But nevertheless Mrs Riordan was constantly on watch, sensitive to any abrasive note that might crop up.

When they had noisily demolished the main meal – with scrupulous sharing of the stuffing from the rabbit all round – there was a bit of a break while they waited for the pudding. Joe watched his father pour himself a small beer, then carefully put the cap back on the bottle and replace it in the Coolgardie safe they'd rigged up in place of an ice box.

'How've you been then?' he asked.

His father shrugged and said wryly, 'Good as you can expect. Santa didn't bring anything, but that was on the cards anyway. He left his IOU though, didn't he kids?'

'Yeah, look,' said young Jimmy, displaying a piece of paper proudly. 'It says right here . . . IOU to the value of fifteen shillings! And it's signed by Father Christmas hisself. He left one for all us kids.'

The others showed their pledges from Santa and young Emily said, 'Father Christmas had a bad year, too. Just like everybody.'

'I know how he feels,' said Joe. 'I couldn't manage a present for everybody, so I just got a special one for Mum. Only a small one, really, but sort of from all of us.'

He produced a wonderfully exotic smelling cake of toilet soap and presented it to her, while the rest of the kids crowded round to admire and wish her a special Christmas.

Mrs Riordan sniffed happily. 'Thank you, Joe. Thank you all.'

'Can I wash my face with it?' pleaded young Emily, sniffing the fragrance.

''Course you can,' said their mum.

John Riordan was very matter of fact about it when he said, 'I been told there's some jobs starting up in Blacktown in February. One of them could be for me.'

Joe was careful to be equally matter of fact in his query, 'Would we have to . . . live out there?'

His father really didn't want to get involved in this aspect of it. 'Well . . . maybe,' he hedged.

His mother cut in crisply, 'There is another way. You could go out every morning on the train. And I could still take in washing.'

'You've already been scrubbing floors, haven't you, Mum?' Joe asked.

'And lucky to get that with times like they are,' said his mother in a tone that made it clear she'd have no more discussion about it.

'Dunno what's happened to the world,' said his father. 'They reckon it's all to do with how that fellow Churchill in England stuck to the Gold Standard. Can't see how that affects it meself.'

'Not just that,' said Joe, quick to take up the theme. 'You gotta remember how the banks foreclosed all over America on the farmers and grocers who couldn't pay up. And there was no more money to spend, anyway.'

'Yeah, of course there was that too,' his father conceded. 'And it was the same story here as well. Don't get me wrong, Joe. I'm not your rabid capitalist. But I know this about the bolshie mob . . . All revolutions end up in dictatorship. You gotta work with the system, or you get anarchy. You can't change the system – except for something worse.'

'Well, I think you can,' said Joe levelly.

A touch of the old antagonism flared up.

'And I'm damned sure you can't,' his father

growled. 'And remember, I've been alive a lot longer than you have.'

Alert to the danger signs, Mrs Riordan cut brusquely in.

'I don't want this conversation to continue,' she said sharply. 'It's Christmas.'

After a pause, John Riordan asked diffidently: 'How you livin', son?'

Joe shrugged, 'Aw, all right. I'm getting by.'

His father pursued the theme delicately. 'Bill Crabtree tells me you've been having a shower down the newspaper office. But he says he doesn't know where you sleep of nights.'

'He's sleeping in the parks, that's where,' said Mrs Riordan with deep feeling.

'I don't want you to do that, son,' said his father. He took a deep breath and added, 'I'd like you to come home.'

Joe's response sounded harsher than he intended.

'I'll come home when I'm good and ready. I'm learning a lot out there.'

His father sighed. 'I'll bet you are.' He looked at Joe, and when he spoke it was not in the tone of parent to child but of one man to another. 'I want to say I'm sorry.'

Joe was touched and disturbed. 'You don't have to be,' he mumbled.

'Christmas pudding!' cried Mrs Riordan, bearing the steaming creature in to excited exclamations from the children.

Both father and son were glad enough of the diversion.

When Joe left late that evening to the clamorous farewells and good wishes of his brothers and sisters, he wore clean clothes and carried a small canvas bag with a change of clothes in it.

'Come back soon,' his mother urged.

'I will. I will.'

'Promise?'

'Yeah, I promise.'

She kissed him goodbye and his father, who had stood back during the farewells, put out his big hand.

'See you, son. Good luck.'

The handshake was between equals, and Joe was a little red-eyed as he walked quickly away down the street without looking back.

CHAPTER 10

The weather had been so balmy that Joe could see no percentage at all in wasting money on the Palace. So he was caught along with many of the other homeless of the city when the cold snap and freak storm swept over in the middle of the night.

The temperature plummeted and the rain poured down. Driven from the park, he huddled with other castaways in the portico of the post office. Sodden, cold and miserable.

He was aching with the beginnings of influenza as he made the morning round and by the time he came to his stand in the street he was feverish. He began to cough and sneeze in the middle of his newsboy call, achieving a completely new variation, which went something like 'Pyer-*choo*!'

'Bless you,' said an old lady passing by.

'Danks,' muttered Joe glumly. He really did need a blessing of some kind.

Reluctantly he expended hardearned money to get into the Palace and spent the night huddled restlessly under the thin blankets. He came out next morning with a high fever – alternately freezing and burning up. He was shivering so violently that his teeth chattered and people looked at him oddly in the street.

One man paused to ask him, 'You all right, mate?'

With his eyes streaming and his head so thick that he could scarcely breathe, Joe managed to gasp, 'Yeah . . . thanks . . I'm fine.'

But he knew he wasn't fine at all. And he knew that this had gone too far for stubbornness and pride to prevail.

When his mother opened the door for him, she let out a wounded cry: 'What's wrong, love?'

'I'm sick, Mum,' he mumbled. 'Can I come home for a bit?'

He swayed in the doorway, and might have fallen if she had not sprung forward, gathering him in her loving arms and supporting him into the house.

It was the flu, the doctor said, and there wasn't much they could do about it. There were no miracle drugs about that could cure it and people still had terrifying memories of the great epidemics of flu that had swept round Australia, and the rest of the world, not all that many years before, killing millions.

Nothing could be done except keep the patient warm and try to ease the congestion and give some relief in breathing. Get a few mouthfuls of broth into him, the doctor had said, and water for the parched throat.

Joe was aware of his mother seeming to always be in attendance at his bedside. When in his delirium he began to shiver and cry out that he was cold – freezing – she was there to tuck more blankets about him. Though of course a few minutes later he would be burning hot and aching all over and struggling desperately for breath.

On the second night the crisis came. The fever broke, and when Joe woke next morning, though still aching and terribly weak, he was immeasurably better. His mother brought him in a bowl of steaming water with a strong solution of eucalyptus in it. She draped a towel over his head and the bowl, so that he could inhale the aromatic fumes to clear the congestion. She smoothed the blankets and plumped up the pillows.

'You may be feeling a bit better, young man,' she told him, 'but you'll stay in bed till I tell you to get up. Everything's under control. I've rung that Mr O'Brien at the paper and he says not to worry. Your job's right and he doesn't expect to see you before Friday at the earliest. Mr Crabtree says the same and he's fixing someone to do your morning round till you're better.'

He would wake briefly and then fall back into exhausted sleep again. His mother seemed to know by some instinct when his eyes opened and would be at the bedside a moment later. From time to time one of his brothers or sisters would come to whisper . . . how was he, and was there anything they could bring him?

Once the eldest of his brothers, young Andrew, was there wanting to talk to him.

'Joe,' he whispered urgently. 'Joe!' And when he saw he was awake and listening he continued. 'I reckon I could leave school and get a job, too, Joe. Like you. I could sell papers or mow lawns or clip hedges or stuff like that.'

'Don't be a mug,' Joe advised him wearily. 'You can't go out working.'

'Well, why do *you* have to?' Andrew demanded.

'I just have to, that's all.'

'I don't see why you can and I can't. It's not fair.'

Joe explained with patience.

'You can't leave school and go out to work because you're too young. I can because I'm nearly fourteen. If anyone's got to go out to work to keep the family going, *I* have to because I'm the eldest.'

Another time he heard sounds of play from the small backyard and got up shakily to go to the window. Looking down, he saw his father passing a football to the other kids, who were spread out around the yard.

Each one clamoured for attention. 'Me! Me! Let me have it, Dad!'

His father faked passes, then tossed it unexpectedly to one or other of them. He laughed loudly when young Jimmy, who had shouted loudest of all, completely muffed the ball and took it on his nose when it actually came to him.

Joe looked down and smiled. You could almost feel affection for your old man when you saw him like this, couldn't you?

It was late in the night when he awoke and found his father standing by the bedside. Joe got the impression he might have been standing there quite a while, waiting.

'You know it's good to see you home again, son?'

Joe was grudging in his reply. 'Just till I get better.'

'Whatever you say, Joe,' said his father equably. 'Just something I wanted to tell you. I signed the pledge by way of a New Year resolution. And I'll stick by it.'

Joe was impressed and disturbed – knowing how dearly his dad loved a beer.

'You didn't have to do that!' he protested.

His father smiled at him seriously, and a bit wryly.

'Oh yes I did, son. And there's something

else I have to show you, or I'd like to show you, at least.'

He produced a photograph. A small photograph with the sepia tint of fading age in it. It showed a small curlyhaired boy wearing a self-conscious grin and holding a handknitted cardigan up as though to display it.

'That's me,' John Riordan told his son. 'After Dad died Mum used to knit things and I had to go round and sell them – or try to sell'm – door to door. It was all we had to live on. That's the earliest picture of me. A bloke took it for free.'

'How old were you?' asked Joe quietly.

'Five,' said his father.

Together they looked at the old photograph – one coming to grips with a new dimension of understanding, the other remembering.

'That was the depression of the nineties,' said John Riordan. 'Things were hard, then. It seemed like the end of the world. I never thought it'd come round again. But it has – and I'm trapped in it again.'

'I'm sorry, Dad,' said Joe softly.

'You don't have to be,' said his father gruffly, but the tone showed he was glad of it.

'I just didn't understand,' said Joe.

CHAPTER 11

The first full day back at work Joe tried to do too much. He was pale still, and not as strong as might be, but stubbornly determined.

Perhaps he was trying to prove something by doing even more than usual. After the morning delivery and the street selling and a bit of a go at the shoe-shine, he found himself on a corner down near Central station trying to sell the communist paper, *Tribune*. He hadn't really wanted to, but he'd promised Jack some time before that he'd take a turn.

He was bone-tired and more than a bit wheezy as he cried: '*Tribune! Tribune!* Get the worker's paper. Inside story of the Lang sacking!'

No one seemed to want the inside story much. 'Ah, stuff it,' he said and was about to give it away, when a well-dressed man in his thirties came up. A sleek sort of a chap with a flower in his button-hole. He had been watching Joe speculatively for a while before approaching him.

'How much?' he asked pleasantly.

'Tuppence,' said Joe.

The man handed over two shillings, and glanced at the headlines as Joe got the change.

'You believe in all this, do you?'

'Yes, I do,' declared Joe as stoutly as he could manage.

The man smiled. 'Well, maybe you could convert me. Like a cup of coffee?'

Suddenly that seemed like a very good idea.

The shop was warm and filled with tantalizing spicy smells and aromas. The customers seemed to Joe to be pretty toffily dressed and there was a lot of laughter and whispering together at small, dimly lit tables.

The man ordered coffee and cakes and talked entertainingly on minor matters. But worn out by his long day, Joe's head drooped and he began to nod. His new acquaintance's manner became more confidential.

'Life – to me – is a desolate thing,' he said. 'But there are small moments of pleasure possible in it.' He regarded Joe keenly. 'But you have to pay for them, of course. You have to pay for everything in the end.'

Joe slurred his agreement. 'That's right, y'do.'

'Maybe you'd like to come back to my place,' the man suggested. 'We could talk about the revolution.'

Joe was suddenly suspicious and alert.

'We can talk about it here,' he said.

'Five shillings?' the man suggested.

'What for? To talk about communism?'

He smiled ambiguously. 'Oh well . . . for a start.'

'No thanks,' said Joe, starting to rise.

'Six shillings,' the man whispered urgently.

'Ah, in your boot,' said Joe roughly.

He stopped at the counter and put a shilling down.

'I'll pay for my own,' he said.

It was late by the time he got home and he was a little surprised to find his father still up. John Riordan sat at the kitchen table with an unopened bottle of beer in front of him.

'It's all right,' he assured Joe. 'I'm not going to drink it. It's just a sort of symbol.'

'What's wrong?' asked Joe.

'The Blacktown job. They didn't want me. Said I was too highly qualified. I offered to work for less, but they said they had principles. They didn't operate like that. Mongrels.'

He brooded for a moment, and then said, 'But what I really waited up to tell you was that I signed on for the dole. I never thought I could bring myself to it . . . But I did.'

Joe had an idea what this meant to his father.

'You didn't have to,' he said. 'I'm doing pretty well. I can keep on working.'

'You're going back to school,' his father declared. 'Somehow or other you're going back, and on to high school. It's the only fair thing.'

'Maybe,' said Joe, with some of the wisdom he had acquired in the past few weeks. 'But you don't often get what's a fair thing these days.'

Perhaps it was the nagging feeling about the chances of getting a fair go that prompted him to go down the street to the stand where the small newsboy was plying his trade.

'Pye-*er*-up! Hinkler vanishes into the blue. Reedawlabartit! Pye-er-*up!*'

He broke off and eyed Joe nervously. 'You just lay off me,' he warned. 'Whatta you want this time?'

Joe tried a reassuring smile. 'Take it easy. I just want to come to an arrangement with you.'

'Oh yeah,' cried the other boy derisively. 'I know all about arrangements. I'm always the one that comes out on the wrong end of them.'

'No, no,' Joe protested. 'This is simple and straightforward. A fair go.' He took a penny out of his pocket. 'Every day I'll toss you to see who gets my pitch. It's the best stand. If I lose, I'll work this pitch for the day.'

The smaller boy looked at him with his mouth wide open.

'What would you want to do that for?' he asked in wonderment.

'I don't think it's fair that I should get the best

pitch all the time. I don't think it's fair you should get the rough end just because you're little.'

The smaller boy thought about it, and came to an inevitable conclusion.

'You must be off your nut,' he said.

Joe grinned and balanced the coin on his thumb. 'For tomorrow,' he said.

'Tails,' claimed the other. Not really believing it.

Joe tossed, and they bent together to inspect the coin where it fell.

'You get the best pitch tomorrow,' said Joe.

'Thanks,' said the smaller boy. But his tone implied that though he'd actually seen it, he still didn't really believe it.

But the next evening, when they'd finished selling, they celebrated the success of the new partnership with a creaming soda at the milk-bar. And the smaller boy, whose name was Fred Atkins, was encouraged to tell Joe something of his own circumstances.

In fact he told it all in one rush, as though it had all been bottled up for a long time and he had been bursting to tell someone.

'Dad cleared off and left us flat,' said Fred. 'There's seven of us. We live with Grandma and she gets the old-age pension. Mum scrubs floors. She took out an order and now Dad's in gaol for not supporting us. I went to see him and called him a mongrel for leaving us.'

Fred took the quickest of sips at his drink and went on rapidly, as though afraid someone might interrupt.

'He cried and cried. Said he'd heard there was a gold strike in Queensland and he'd gone off so he could come back with a fortune. A fortune for all of us. But when he got there it was all staked out and he had to come back riding the rattler. And he got caught and put in gaol and he rang Grandma for the bail money, but she wouldn't part up. And when he served his time and got back here, Mum had worked out how much maintenance he owed. And now he's in the choky because he didn't pay it. And every week he's in gaol it's a week's more maintenance he owes. And he reckons there's no way he can win.'

Fred Atkins was forced to pause to draw breath. And Joe, overwhelmed, could only say, 'Crikey.'

'I reckon my dad's not such a bad sort of bloke really,' said Fred tolerantly. 'But Mum won't have a bar of him. Not any more. Says he's a weakie.'

'That's tough,' said Joe. 'Have another creaming soda. My shout.'

Fred looked at him suspiciously.

'You're not a mad Christian or anything like that, are you?'

'Not me,' said Joe.

CHAPTER 12

When he got home his parents were waiting for him, and his mother put the question directly, 'Do you want to go back to school, Joe?'

His heart leapt at the prospect, but he had to face facts.

'Well, I can't, can I?' he said evasively.

'We think you've done your bit,' said his father. 'Much more than your bit. We've decided to move in with your grandma.'

Joe was appalled. 'What, all of us?'

'Don't think we've got any choice, son.'

Joe was distressed and defeated.

'But . . . everything I did . . . it was to keep us here. To keep us together – at home.'

'There's no other way,' his father assured him, equally distressed. 'It's only fair that you go back to school – that you get some sort of a chance. And we can't work it any other way.'

'Doesn't seem to be very fair to me,' said Joe.

When he tossed Fred Atkins for the top pitch next day, he told him: 'Not to worry. It'll be all yours soon.'

Fred looked at him shrewdly.

'Going back to school, then, are you?'

'Yeah,' said Joe.

Fred was embarrassed at the possibility of showing sentimentality.

'Well, come and see a bloke sometime,' he said gruffly. 'I'll be round here somewhere.'

'Sure,' said Joe. 'But I might be caught up in other jobs y'know. And high school's across the other side of town.'

'Yeah, sure,' said Fred. 'I know how it is.'

On the way home he bumped into Robbo and told him the news. His old schoolmate was delighted at the prospect of Joe returning to the fold. But his first thought, naturally, was for just one thing.

'Bewdy!' he said. 'Now we'll be able to get you back on the cricket team. We need you bad.'

Joe smiled to himself. Robbo was certainly dedicated to the game. But just the same it would be good to get back into the fold. Jeez. How long was it since he'd held a cricket ball in his hand?

Then on top of this, he walked into the Riordan establishment to find everything transformed. Instead of the gloomy household he had last seen, preparing for the move to Grandma's, he found a family celebration in full swing.

'What happened?' he asked, bewildered, as they dragged him into the noisy kitchen.

Everyone seemed to be talking at once, but finally he managed to make out what it was his father was telling him. And John Riordan told it all in a rush, without pausing for breath, very much the way Fred Atkins had done.

'Well, you see I went out to Blacktown and I told him what happened – about you and everything – and I told him that in my view it was fairer to take a qualified man on lower wages than to deprive his family of a proper home and his eldest son of schooling.

'I told him I had principles, too. I tell you I argued most forcibly. And finally he said I'd have to pretend I wasn't qualified – that I'd deceived him – and he'd take me on.

'You know what? I absolutely agreed! I gotta get up at five-thirty in the damn morning to sit in a train for an hour to get there by eight o'clock . . . and it'll be damn miserable and rotten cold . . . and I've never been happier in my whole life!'

It finally dawned on Joe.

'You mean we can stay here?'

'My oath we can,' said his father. 'The family stays together. And you can go on to high school. And never mind about waiting till March the first for it to be Christmas day. Christmas is the Friday after next! Santa keeps his word – and so do I!'

Which is how it happened that, long after everyone else had celebrated, the Riordans sat down to their Christmas dinner.

The little kitchen was gaily decorated with streamers and they all had presents wrapped in brightly coloured paper, and wore party hats.

Mrs Riordan had borrowed a record of Christmas carols which were playing on the old phonograph in the other room as they ate their Christmas dinner.

It wasn't exactly a leg of ham this time, either. But there was pickled pork, wasn't there? And stuffed chicken with roast potatoes. And another, richer pudding, with lashings of sauce and a big sprig of holly on the top.

Joe could hear the words of the carol . . . *Away in the manger, no crib for a bed* . . . Well, he knew a lot about that, didn't he? He'd learned a lot out there battling in the streets when he'd had nowhere to lay his head.

On an impulse, he lifted his glass of creaming soda and turned to his father.

'Good on you, Dad,' he said. 'Cheers.'

John Riordan lifted his own glass.

'Cheers,' he said. 'You know I'm proud of you, son.'

Joe looked round at all the other laughing, loving and excited faces . . . and knew that it had all been worthwhile.